KT-497-838

Baby on Board

Allan Ahlberg

Illustrated by Emma Chichester Clark

PUFFIN

Once, many years ago,
there was a baby
in his pram,
with his sisters
and their sandwiches and lemonade
and toys,
and their friends
and a kite,
and a dog or two . . .

THE ROYAL BOROUGH OF
KINGSTON
UPON THAMES

...ces

uk/libraries

Request a book
Email a branch
Get your pin
free reference sites

06

mes

KT 2346176 4

PUFFIN BOOKS

UK | USA | Canada | Ireland | Australia | India | New Zealand | South Africa
Puffin Books is part of the Penguin Random House group of companies
whose addresses can be found at global.penguinrandomhouse.com.

www.penguin.co.uk   www.puffin.co.uk   www.ladybird.co.uk

 Penguin
Random House
UK

First published 2018
Published in this edition 2019
001

Text copyright © Allan Ahlberg, 2018
Illustrations copyright © Emma Chichester Clark, 2018

The moral right of the author and illustrator has been asserted

Printed in China

A CIP catalogue record for this book is available from the British Library

ISBN: 978–0–241–38543–2

All correspondence to:
Puffin Books, Penguin Random House Children's
80 Strand, London WC2R 0RL

MIX
Paper from
responsible sources
FSC
www.fsc.org   FSC® C018179

. . . on the beach.

All that sunny morning
the children played
and took good care of the baby.

They made a den with some deckchairs
and ate their sandwiches
and drank their lemonade.

Only then, later on when the kite string broke,
they ran and followed the kite,
every one of them ~
it was only natural, really ~

and *forgot* the baby.

And the pram began to **move**.

And the tide came **rolling in**.

And the baby clapped
his little hands
and laughed . . .

. . . and sailed away.

The baby ~ luckily ~ was not alone.
Three of his sisters' favourite toys
were there in the pram with him,
all drifting out upon the open sea.

The panda and the doll
watched over the baby.
(The poor old rabbit was seasick.)
They gave him his bottle
and tucked him in
when the wind began to blow,
and wiped his face
when the waves began to splash.

Only then, quite soon,
the waves and wind got larger and louder,
and turned . . .

. . . into a **storm!**

The baby frowned
and clutched his special bit of flannel
and sucked his thumb,

while the panda and the doll ~
and the rabbit now ~
worked **frantically** to keep the pram afloat . . .

. . . till the storm passed.

The pram sailed on.
Warm breezes dried its blankets
and its pillow and its baby
and its crew.

The happy baby ate a banana,
drank some juice
from his little cup,
played 'Peepo'
with the panda and the doll . . .

and dozed.

Only then ~ whoosh! ~

a young and curious puffin
landed on the handle
of the pram,
startling the doll,
scaring the rabbit,
delighting the baby.
"Da!" he cried
and pointed at the bird.

Only *then*, more excited still,
the baby flung
his little podgy arms out wide

and knocked the poor old panda
overboard!

Now the rabbit and the doll
worked frantically to save the panda.

Luckily, all animals can swim,
even toy ones,
or float, for a time at least

until their clever and determined friends
can work out what to do . . .

and throw them a line . . .

and haul them in.

The pram sailed on.
The sun sank lower in the sky.
The dozy *smelly* baby
lolled back on his pillow.
The rabbit sneezed.

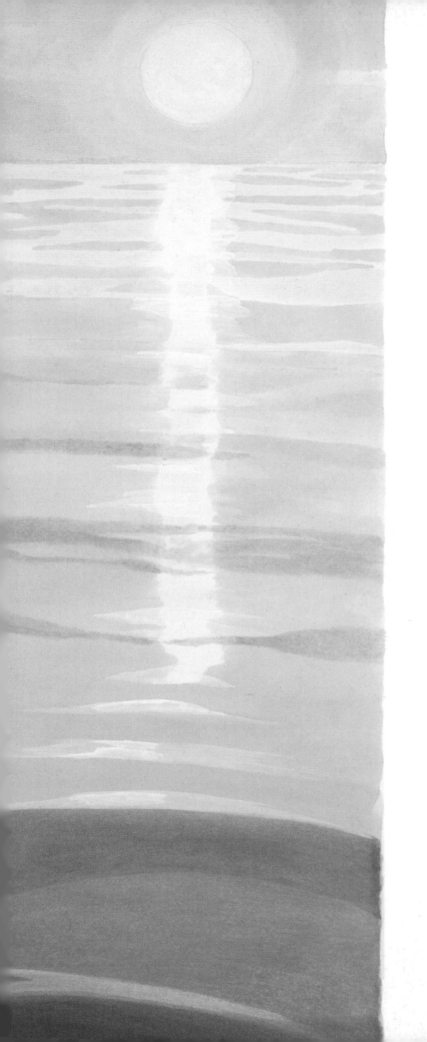

All of a sudden ~

it was the strangest thing ~

the pram began to jerk about,
this way and that,

hurling spray into the air
and churning through the water
like a speedboat.

They had a **huge** *fish* on their line
or, nearer to the truth perhaps,
the fish had them . . .
till the line **broke.**

Night,
and a scatter of silver stars
and a sliver of moon
and a dazzling, swinging beam of light
from the lighthouse.

Up onto the silent beach
came the pram.
Only then,
half in and half out of the water,
it ground to a halt
and would not budge.

The panda and the rabbit,
though each of them was quite worn out,
went running off to look for help,

across the sand

and **up** the steps

and **down** the street

and **into** the gardens

and up to the doors and windows of the darkened houses.

So it was
that the toys of the town
came out to help . . .

and *heave*...

HOORAY!

After that, the final scene:
footsteps and torches on the beach,
barking and shouts of joy.

The baby was back
with his sisters again,
and his mum and his dad,
and his grandmas and grandpas,
uncles and aunties,
neighbours and friends,
and a dog or two . . .

Safe and sound.